CHEESE FROM DIMENSION PONG

Dedicated to Wilf and Rafe
-JPG

For my sister Jackie and her very own pet defenders,
Yogi, Mia and Tai.
-SM

STRIPES PUBLISHING
An imprint of the Little Tiger Group
1 Coda Studios, 189 Munster Road,
London SW6 6AW

A paperback original
First published in Great Britain in 2018

Text copyright © Gareth P. Jones, 2018
Illustrations copyright © Steve May, 2018

ISBN: 978-1-84715-944-1

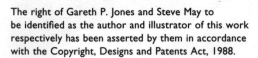

Printed and bound in the UK.

10 9 8 7 6 5 4 3 2 1

PET DEFENDERS

CHEESE FROM DIMENSION PONG

GARETH P. JONES

ILLUSTRATED BY
STEVE MAY

Stripes

PET DEFENDERS

Protecting those who protect us

Did you know that Earth is under constant alien attack?

Don't worry.

We are the Pet Defenders, a secret society of domestic animals. We are your dogs, cats, rabbits and rodents. While you are off at school or work or doing whatever it is you humans do, we are keeping the Earth safe.

We keep our work hidden because we know what humans are like. The first sight of an Atomic Burp or a Drizzle-eyed Lizzle-Flicker and you'll panic.

TOP SECRET

Before you know it, you'll have blown up the very planet we're trying to defend.

Just carry on as normal — stroke your cats, take your dogs for walks and clean out your hamster cages. Don't forget to feed us, but please … let *us* take care of the aliens.

Now that you know all this, we need you to forget it. Our specially trained seagulls will take care of that. Ah, here they are with the Forget-Me-Plop now…

SSSPLAT!

CHAPTER 1

MARTIN THE MARTIAN MARSHMALLOW

It was a cold blustery Saturday and every bench along Nothington-on-Sea's promenade was empty. The bins, however, were full of chip wrappers, empty drinks cans and other bits of rubbish. But one of them also included a scruffy mongrel called Biskit and a tabby cat by the name of Mitzy.

The Pet Defenders' day had started when a small squishy-headed Martian had surprised a scout group on a campsite by leaping out of the undergrowth and running off with a bag of marshmallows.

While a squadron of trained seagulls wiped the witnesses' memories with Forget-Me-Plop, Biskit and Mitzy had followed the mischievous alien into town, before finally capturing it inside an empty takeaway box.

"This isn't fair," complained the creature, kicking his spindly arms and legs against the box. "I'm scared of enclosed spaces."

"You're scared? How do you think those scouts felt?" replied Mitzy.

"They were burning my people's heads on sticks in that brutal ritual of theirs," squeaked the Martian.

"We've been through this," sighed Mitzy. "Those things were not Martians. They were marshmallows."

"Quiet, both of you," said Biskit, sniffing. "He's close now."

Mitzy peered out of the bin and saw the

patchy red fur of an urban fox walking along the promenade, carefully inspecting each bin.

"Who is that?" she asked.

"His name is Daley," said Biskit. "I think that he's the one who suggested this marshmallow-headed Martian take his holiday on a campsite."

"Let me out," said the alien.

"OK, but only so you can identify him." Mitzy lifted her paw off the box and the alien's soft head slowly emerged. It looked so like a marshmallow that Mitzy had to resist the urge to have a lick to see whether it tasted like one. The alien clambered up the inside of the bin and looked out.

"Yes, that's him, all right," he said.

"So Daley's back to his old tricks, is he?" said Biskit.

"What tricks? I've never heard of him," said Mitzy.

"That's because he retired before you moved here. Or rather, he was supposed to have retired." Biskit placed a paw on the Martian's head and pushed him back down.

The alien resisted him. "I'm not going back in that box. It smells of chicken and I've got breadcrumbs stuck in all sorts of places now."

"We can't allow you to be seen," said Biskit.

"I don't care," said the alien. "It's not right, you treating me like this. I'm on holiday."

Without warning, the small alien sprang out of the bin, startling the fox, who was up on his hind legs trying to retrieve something from another bin. Biskit and Mitzy followed the Martian into the open.

"Stop where you are," ordered Mitzy.

The alien hopped on to a low wall. It teetered and waved its arms to keep its balance. "Why? So you can put me back in a box? Not likely."

"You do not want to fall off that wall," said Mitzy. "There's a three-metre drop to the pebble beach on the other side and Earth's gravity is much stronger than on Mars. Fall off and there won't even be enough of you left to toast."

Daley turned to look at the Martian. "She's right. It's not worth it."

"I won't go back in the box," said the Martian.

"OK, we promise not to put you back in a box," said Mitzy.

The small alien climbed down from the wall, only for Biskit to leap up, snatch a plastic bag that was rolling past and then scoop him up.

"Hey," protested the alien.

"I'm sorry, but we can't risk anyone seeing you," said Mitzy.

"That's him all wrapped up then," said Daley. "I'd better be off." He turned to leave, only to find that Biskit was sitting on his tail.

"What have you been up to, Daley?" asked Biskit.

"Minding my own business," he replied.

Biskit smiled. "Yeah, well, now it's Pet Defenders' business and you're not going anywhere until you start talking."

CHAPTER 2

DALEY THE FOX

"Daley," snarled Biskit, "you no-good, flea-ridden bag of bones."

"It's good to see you, too, Biskit," said the fox, pulling his tail free and jumping up to stick his nose in another bin, then pulling out a half-eaten supermarket sandwich.

Before he could take a bite, Biskit snatched it off him. "First you talk, then you eat," he growled.

Daley sighed. "Hey, the last time I saw you, Champ fell through a portal."

"We're not here to talk about his ex-partner," said Mitzy. "I'm his new one."

"A dog and cat partnership. How's *that* working out?" asked Daley.

"It's fine," said Biskit. "Right now, I'm more worried about a certain fox who promised he was going to stay away from portals."

"Yeah, well, a fox has got to eat," said Daley with a shrug.

"I don't understand," said Mitzy.

"A portal is a gateway to another part of the universe. They appear in weak spots in the fabric of reality," said Daley.

"Yes, I know that," said Mitzy. "What have they got to do with you?"

Biskit kept his eyes on Daley as he answered Mitzy. "Daley can sniff out portals that appear."

"Actually, it's not smelling," said Daley. "I lost my sense of smell as a cub. It's more like I sense them, if you know what I mean. It's hard to explain."

"How's that possible?" asked Mitzy.

"No idea. Call me gifted," said Daley.

"Yes, but Champ and I discovered he was hanging out by portals then getting to aliens before we did," said Biskit. "Instead of sending them straight back, he was helping them find places to hide here on Earth."

"Why? What do you get out of it?" asked Mitzy.

"Food," said Daley. "They would bring me their local delicacies and, in return, I used to help them find their way around. I've given all that up now, though."

"So how do you explain the Martian in this bag?" asked Biskit.

"What? Him? He's harmless," said Daley.

"Tell that to the First Nothington Scout Group," said Biskit.

"Yes, you seriously endangered the town and the planet by allowing this thing in," said Mitzy.

"This *thing*?" cried the Martian. "I do have a name, you know. I'm called Martin."

"Martin the Marshmallow Martian?" said Mitzy.

Daley sniggered. "You Pet Defenders always assume that every visiting alien is trying to take over our planet," he said. "Most of them are just sightseeing. I point them in the right direction and tell them how to avoid getting seen. You should thank me."

Daley reached a paw to get the sandwich but Biskit bared his teeth at him. "How many more?"

"Martin was a one-off, I swear," said Daley.

"Tell me the truth," said Biskit.

"I swear on this sandwich," said Daley. "I'm out of the game now. Why do you think I'm foraging for myself around here?" He reached to get the sandwich and this time Biskit allowed him to take it, then placed his paw down on it again as Daley was about to tuck in.

"If you're lying to me—" Biskit began.

Daley growled in frustration. "Listen, us street animals don't get our food delivered in a bowl like you two."

"You don't know me," said Mitzy, a little anger showing in her eyes. "I've lived on the streets."

Daley sniggered bitterly. "Yeah, and then you rubbed yourself against the legs of some gullible human and got taken in, did you?"

"Philip gave her a home because he's kind,"

said Biskit.

"Philip? Your owner?" Daley looked at Biskit and laughed. "You got your owner to adopt her? Oh, hilarious. You've let a cat move in? What's that like? Is it true what they say about their bottom smells?"

Biskit grinned. "It can get a little whiffy after dinner," he admitted.

"You can talk," said Mitzy. "After a packet of Barkin' Bites it's like being trapped in a wind tunnel."

"Well, I think it's sweet – alien-fighting partners and flatmates," said Daley, finally taking a bite of the sandwich. "You make a lovely couple."

"So can I go now?" said Martin.

"The only place you're going is straight through a portal and back to Mars," said Biskit.

"I could help you with that," said Daley. "In fact, there's one not far from here—"

"You are under strict instructions to stay away from portals," said Biskit. "Example One's lab mice will get this Martian back home."

Mitzy nodded at a nearby seagull on the wall. The large white bird swooped down and snatched the bag containing Martin in its beak, then took off into the sky.

WAAAAAAAH!

"Waaaaaah," yelled Martin as the seagull carried him over the houses and shops of Nothington-on-Sea.

"Poor thing," said Daley. "Trapped in a bag on his holiday."

"So it's a package holiday," said Biskit with a smile.

"It may seem cruel," said Mitzy, "but if humans learned how often aliens were arriving on their planet there would be mass panic. As Pet Defenders it is our duty to stop that from happening."

"OK, I'm just saying the universe is a big interesting place," said Daley. "Would it hurt for you to be a bit more welcoming?"

Biskit growled. "Just stay away from portals and leave the alien stuff to the professionals."

"Of course," said Daley. "But Biskit, keep an eye on this cat. Losing one partner is unlucky. Losing two would be careless."

CHAPTER 3

...

NEVILLE THE PUG

The Pet Defenders made their way across town quickly, quietly and out of sight from the humans. It had been a long day and they were both keen to get home.

"I'm so hungry," said Biskit. "I can't wait to eat."

"Yes, and remember that Philip said his mother was coming to visit today," said Mitzy.

They were running along a narrow wall between a playground and a small park. Biskit stopped so suddenly that Mitzy almost ran into him.

"What is it?" she said.

"Philip's mother hates me," he moaned, his tail dropping down between his legs.

"Surely not," said Mitzy. "You're so loveable."

"Whenever she visits, it's all, *Oh, Philip, I don't know why you don't get rid of that revolting mutt.*"

Mitzy smiled. "Maybe she's a cat person."

Biskit scowled back. "We need to get in, eat, then get out before she turns up."

Mitzy was still thinking about their conversation with Daley. "You know, that fox was right," she said. "Pets have it easy."

"We're more than pets," said Biskit. "We're Pet Defenders. We might get our food in a bowl but we keep this planet safe."

"Not all aliens arrive here to attack us," said Mitzy, mulling it over. "We can get a bit gung-ho about fighting them off."

"What are you suggesting? That we start welcoming aliens who arrive here? Put them in a hotel?"

"No, I don't know what I'm saying. Maybe just that we shouldn't always assume the worst." She jumped off the wall on to a tree branch, which bowed under her weight and lowered her to the ground. She stepped off and it swung back up.

Biskit followed her. He was about to respond when they heard barking.

He turned to see a pug running towards them. He had one wonky ear and a pink tongue that dangled out of his mouth as his little legs moved double-time.

"Someone, help. Help me!"

"HELP!

HELP!"

"Calm down." Biskit's bark silenced the pug. "What's your name and what is the matter?"

The pug stared at him for a moment with his tongue flopped over his lower lip. He was slow to respond, as though it took a long time for his brain to tell his body what to do. Finally he said, "My name is Neville and it's my owners. They've both been knocked out. I can't wake them up. I don't understand what's going on."

"Show us," said Mitzy.

The pug led Biskit and Mitzy across the park to a shady spot with a picnic bench covered in a checkered tablecloth and with a wicker hamper. The jug of lemonade had been knocked over, spilling yellow liquid across the tablecloth. Both of the pug's owners lay slumped over the table, their heads lying in their plates of food.

"It was supposed to be a breakfast picnic," said Neville. "I went to chase pigeons. When I came back they were like this. Please! You have to help them."

Biskit didn't hesitate. He immediately set about sniffing everything he could, searching for clues. It looked as though the humans had knocked various things off the table when they collapsed. A half-eaten baguette lay on the ground next to an upside-down tub of butter.

A couple of wasps buzzed around a jam jar that lay on its side.

"Anything?" asked Mitzy.

"Yes, crusty bread," said Biskit, taking a bite from the baguette. "Yum."

"Hey, that's not yours," said Neville. "I thought you were going to help me."

Biskit licked his lips. "We are going to help, but I'm starving and I work better on a full stomach." Biskit followed a scent to a large hardback book lying on the ground. He nudged open the cover with his nose and saw that some pages had been hollowed out.

"There was something in here."

"What sort of something?" said Neville. "What did this?"

The humans shifted in their sleep. "No, no, too crumbly. Too mature," muttered the man.

"Ah, please stop. So runny and so strong…" moaned the woman.

Neither opened their eyes.

"What's wrong with them?" asked Neville.

"They appear to be dreaming," said Mitzy.

"WAKE UP!" barked Biskit at the top of his voice.

"Not the mould…" muttered the man, still asleep.

Biskit jumped up on to the bench, picked up the man's sleeve in his teeth, then dropped it. The man's hand flopped down.

"Too mild, too blue…" he said.

"Now, Neville –" Mitzy turned to the pug – "we need to know what occurred before your owners collapsed."

"I told you, I was running after pigeons. I didn't see a thing."

Mitzy prowled around the scene, looking for clues, while Biskit sniffed the humans' fingers. This time, he followed a scent that led to an open plastic container on the table. There was a packet of biscuits inside. Biskit tried one.

"I prefer ones with chocolate," he said.

"Are you just going to keep stealing food or are you going to do something?" demanded Neville.

Biskit turned to face him. "This isn't eating. It's investigating with my mouth."

At the other end of the table, Mitzy had found a blue waxy case. She tapped it with her paw. "What was in here?" she asked.

"Cheese," said Neville. "My owners love the stuff. She bought this from that cheese shop in town."

"Cheeeese," moaned the two sleeping humans.

Biskit and Mitzy looked at each other, then Biskit looked back at the container. "They're not biscuits. They're cheese crackers," he said.

"Neville, did you see the cheese that was inside?" asked Mitzy.

"No. Why?" asked Neville.

"I think this cheese may have knocked out your owners," said Mitzy.

"If it did, it vanished into thin air afterwards." Biskit ran around in circles. "There's no trail."

"Vanishing cheese?" said Neville. "What are you two talking about? Who are you?"

"Neville, you need to keep calm," said Mitzy. "And trust us."

"Yes, stay here with your owners," said Biskit. "We'll send a squadron of seagulls to help them and to wipe your memory."

"No," said Mitzy. "We need him to take us

to this cheese shop."

"Please, no more cheeeeeese!" groaned the man.

"Whatever was inside that blue wax case, it's clearly dangerous and we need to find the source."

"Cheese sauce," murmured Neville's owners.

Biskit took another cracker from the tub.

"So what did you find out from that one?" Neville yapped.

"I discovered that these crackers are going stale," said Biskit.

"Now we should get cracking," said Mitzy. "Let's go."

CHAPTER 4

❀

SAY CHEESE!

Unlike the Pet Defenders, Neville the pug had never needed to stay out of sight. He led them along the pavements. As they approached one row of shops, a greengrocer and her customer paused to look at the three animals.

"I wonder where they're off to in such a hurry," said the greengrocer, rearranging her lemons.

"Strays probably," said her customer, squeezing an avocado.

"Someone should do something about the animals in this town," said the greengrocer. "And those pesky seagulls, pooping all over the place."

As the pug trotted past them, the humans heard him make a noise that sounded like, "Owf! Owf! Oooowf!" unaware that he was talking to the dog and cat behind him.

"It's my fault," he muttered unhappily. "Curse those wretched pigeons for making me chase them."

"You can't blame yourself," said Mitzy.

"Or the pigeons," added Biskit. "Whatever did that to your owners would have done it to you, too, had you been there."

"But what could it have been?" asked Neville, stopping in his tracks. "I don't understand."

"Biskit and I are Pet Defenders," said Mitzy. "Do you know what that means?"

"No," said Neville.

"You've never heard of us?" said Biskit, a little disappointed.

"Should I have done?" asked the pug.

"It doesn't matter," said Mitzy firmly. "But we do need to keep moving. We're drawing attention to ourselves." She had noticed an elderly man on a mobility scooter who had stopped to look at them barking and meowing at each other.

"It's on this next road, next door to the library," said Neville.

Biskit and Mitzy followed him to a lamppost across the road from a shop called SAY CHEESE!

"Maybe you should wait here, Neville," said Biskit.

"But what are you hoping to find in there?" yapped Neville. "It's just a cheese shop. How is this going to help my owners?"

"Calm down," barked Biskit. "And try to stay quiet."

"We won't be long," said Mitzy.

The Pet Defenders crossed the road and found a couple of plant pots to hide behind. Through the glass door, they could see a man talking to the cheesemonger, while a toddler sat in a pushchair, playing with a cuddly toy.

A taxi pulled up outside and a woman in a large fur coat got out. "Wait here, please," she said. "I need to get some cheese."

"But I'm on a double yellow," said the taxi driver.

"I fail to see how that is my problem," snapped the woman.

Mitzy and Biskit waited until she opened the door, then snuck in behind her. The cheesemonger and his customer didn't notice the dog and cat slip inside the shop and hide under a couple of empty crates. But the toddler pointed at Biskit and said, "Doggy."

"Yes, we've seen lots of dogs today, haven't we, Daniel?" said his dad.

"Oh, don't talk to me about dogs," said the woman. "I'm on my way to see my son. He has a revolting old mutt."

Mitzy looked at Biskit. He nodded. This was Philip's mother.

"Anyway, I'd like to buy some cheese," she said.

"This gentleman was before you," replied the cheesemonger, who wore a white apron pulled tightly over his large belly.

"But I have a taxi on

yellow lines outside," said Philip's mother.

"It's fine, you go first," said the other customer. "I'm still deciding."

"Well, that's very civil of you," she said.

"Hello, meow meow," said the toddler, noticing Mitzy.

Luckily for the Pet Defenders, all three adults ignored him.

"What would you like?" asked the cheesemonger.

"When it comes to cheese, I always say the smellier the better," replied Philip's mother. "Although I am in a bit of a hurry. How about that one?" She pointed at a cheese behind the counter.

"Er. But…" began the cheesemonger.

"Please don't argue with me."

He gave her the cheese and she handed him a

five-pound note, then hurriedly left.

"You get all sorts in here," he said, turning to the other customer. "So, have you decided?"

"No," said the man. "What did she buy?"

"It's a funny thing, but I'm not sure what it was. I don't remember putting that one out."

Mitzy noticed Biskit was standing up and looking out of the window. "Biskit," she whispered. "Stay hidden."

"Doggy doggy," said the toddler.

"There's no d—" his father began, before looking down and seeing Biskit.

"It's the same blue wax case," barked Biskit. "And she's taking it to Philip's."

Mitzy sprang out from her hiding place.

"Hello, meow meow," squealed the toddler.

"No animals in the shop," shouted the cheesemonger.

"Let us out then," barked Biskit.

The humans didn't understand what he was saying but the customer opened the door to shoo them away. The Pet Defenders didn't need shooing. They bolted out to find that the taxi had already gone.

"What's wrong?" asked Neville, joining them. "Have you found out what happened to my owners?"

"No, but the same is about to happen to ours if we don't hurry," said Biskit. "Come on."

CHAPTER 5

FLYING CHEESE

Neville found the world a confusing place at the best of times, but he had absolutely no idea what was going on as he raced to keep up with Biskit and Mitzy. They scampered down alleyways, under hedges and through the back gardens of Nothington-on-Sea, talking as fast as they ran.

"Shouldn't we tell Commander F what's happening?" said Mitzy.

"There's no time." Biskit looked up at a seagull flying overhead. "Anyway, I'm pretty sure he's watching the whole thing."

"What do you think it is?" asked Mitzy.

"I've no idea but whatever it is, if it attacks my owner it's going to regret it," said Biskit.

"*Our* owner," said Mitzy.

They rounded a corner and Neville saw a block of flats. "What are you two talking about? Where are we?"

"Neville," said Mitzy, who had forgotten the pug was still with them. "You should probably wait outside."

"No, I'm staying with you two until I know what knocked out my owners."

The pug followed them up the concrete stairway then through a flap in the door. As he stepped inside, he instantly recognized the smell from when he had returned to the picnic bench. A man he didn't know lay on the carpet next to the lady from the cheese shop.

"Philip, Philip," barked Biskit. "Can you hear me, Philip? It's me, Biskit."

"Too much cheeeeeese," groaned Philip.

"No more cheeeeeese," moaned his mother.

Mitzy picked up an empty waxy blue case and dropped it at Biskit's feet.

"Another missing cheese?" she said.

Biskit darted into the kitchen, then sprang up at the window and looked out. "There," he said.

Neville ran to the window as well. It was too high so he scrambled up and on to a chair to see. Down below was the extraordinary sight of a small round creature hovering just off the ground, moving away from the block of flats.

"That's why it left no scent," said Mitzy. "It can fly."

Biskit jumped on to the windowsill and looked down. "It'll be gone by the time we get there."

"No, Biskit. It's too far," said Mitzy.

"Too far for what? What are you two talking about?" barked Neville.

Biskit ignored him. Instead he turned to Mitzy and said, "Do you know, I think I've realized why I'm scared of heights."

"Why?" asked Mitzy.

"Because I so often end up jumping off them," he replied.

Before Neville could ask what this meant, Biskit jumped out of the window.

"Biskit," meowed Mitzy.

As Biskit plummeted towards the ground, he found himself wishing he had come up with a plan before jumping. There was nothing below to soften his fall. There were no handy bushes, deep puddles or conveniently placed mattresses. Biskit's only chance was to land on top of the creature. He straightened his legs and tail, tucked in his head and arched his body.

He was overshooting so he spread his legs wide in a desperate effort to change direction. The whole thing was over in a matter of seconds but, during that time, Biskit felt his senses heightened. His skin tingled with the thrill of doing something utterly reckless. And then… **FLUH-SPLANG!** Biskit landed on the alien.

The creature was clearly surprised by this and lurched to the side.

"Release me," yelled the alien cheese.

As Biskit clung on, he noticed a small set of eyes and a tiny mouth but it was the smell that hit him hard. It was horrendous, worse than a pair of Philip's old jogging socks left on a compost heap with a pile of dead fish. Biskit felt woozy and confused. He tried to speak but his mouth wouldn't form the words. "I'm with the Det Pefenders... I mean, the Pend Defetters... That's not it... The defriending petters... Er..."

It was no use. The smell was too much. Biskit felt his muscles weaken as the stink overtook all of his other senses. He dropped to the ground with a **THUD-DU-FLUP!** It would have been extremely painful had he been awake to feel it but Biskit's eyes were closed, his nose was twitching and his mind was somewhere else entirely.

In her time as Biskit's partner, Mitzy had watched him cling on to car bumpers, jump off cliffs and drop over waterfalls of snot. Leaping out of their apartment window wasn't the most dangerous thing he had done but Mitzy still feared the day that one of his crazy stunts would end badly. She couldn't watch as he landed on the alien then collapsed to the ground, allowing it to fly away.

"He's been knocked out," said Neville.

Mitzy didn't have time to respond. She was out of the cat flap and down the steps as fast as her legs would carry her. She sped round the side of the building, where she found Biskit lying on the grass, writhing and moaning.

"Please, no cheese…"

"Biskit?" she cried, nudging him with her paw. He shifted and groaned but didn't stir.

Mitzy lifted one of his floppy ears and yelled again, "BISKIT!"

"Our tests so far have shown noise to be of no use," said a familiar voice behind her.

Mitzy spun round to find a bespectacled pink mouse sitting in a saddle attached to a rather large seagull. The seagull squawked and pecked the ground, allowing the mouse to slide down his neck.

Neville stepped back nervously. "Who are you?"

"Oh, hello." The mouse adjusted his glasses. "I'm Example One of the Nothington Extra-terrestrial Research Division (or NERD for short). I've been treating your human owners. I'm very pleased to meet you."

He offered the pug his paw.

Unsure how to respond, Neville edged forwards and licked it. Example One wiped his paw on his tail and took a tiny electronic tablet from the seagull's saddlebag. He then plucked a stylus from behind his ear.

Biskit shifted in his sleep and batted something away with his paw. "Not the fondue."

"Example One," said Mitzy. "Have you any idea what is going on?"

"Yes and no," replied the pink mouse. "Biskit is trapped in a deep sleep, experiencing some kind of cheesy nightmare. Why this is happening, I cannot be sure."

"So how do we wake him?" asked Mitzy.

"I'm still working on that," said Example One. "Have you any idea what did this?"

"It appeared to be some kind of flying cheese," said Mitzy.

"Fascinating," said Example One. "Most probably alien in origin, of course."

"Alien?" said Neville. "What's he talking about?"

"Neville," said Mitzy. "The Pet Defenders monitor alien activity and keep the planet safe from invasion."

"Like in flying saucers, you mean?" Neville looked up at the sky, eyes wide with wonder.

"More often they appear through portals," said Example One.

"Portals?"

"Gateways that appear within the folds of reality, providing shortcuts to other galaxies and different dimensions," said Example One. "We have a lot of them here in Nothington."

"We're wasting time," said Mitzy. "The question is, how do we wake Biskit?" She couldn't bear to see Biskit twitching and muttering about cheese.

Example One looked at Mitzy over the top of his glasses and coughed. "I've never encountered anything like it. I think we need to take him to Barb."

"Who's Barb?" asked Neville.

"A pan-dimensional alien in the form of a fish," Mitzy said casually. She turned back to Example One. "I'll drag Biskit there."

"No need for that," said Example One, typing something into his tablet. "We'll use the airlift seagull squad."

Three burly seagulls flew down and circled Biskit. Instead of saddles, these had harnesses around their bodies. From these harnesses, three lines lowered with hooks that looped themselves round Biskit's head, tummy and hind legs. Then the seagulls angled themselves upwards and lifted Biskit into the air.

Example One scrambled back on to his seagull and yelled, "I'll see you there."

"Where?" asked Neville.
"Where are they taking him?"

"Biskit is sick," said Mitzy. "They're
taking him to the vet's."

CHAPTER 6

🐾

CHEESE FROM DIMENSION PONG

Dr Udall's veterinary surgery was closed on Saturdays so all the doors were locked. Mitzy led Neville round the back, where they found the four seagulls quarrelling over a half-eaten bag of crisps. The window was open.

"I know this place," said Neville. "The last time I was here, the vet put her finger right up—"

"Neville," interrupted Mitzy. "It's probably best if you wait outside."

Mitzy sprang up on to the windowsill with

ease and looked back at the pug. "I won't be long. Stay there."

She jumped into the surgery and saw that Biskit was now lying in the middle of the room, wriggling and murmuring in his disturbed sleep. Example One was making notes on his tablet while the Pet Defenders' white rabbit boss, Commander F, paced back and forth, gnawing a radish top. A bulbous-eyed fish hovered above him, swimming around the bubble of water which floated with it.

"Wow. How's it doing that?"

Mitzy turned round to find that Neville had somehow managed to climb on to the windowsill. The determined pug was staring open-mouthed at the floating fish.

"Who are you?" demanded Commander F.

"This is Neville," said Mitzy. "His owners were knocked out by the cheese."

"Oh, the horror … the horror … the horrible cheese," muttered Biskit.

"Barb, have you any idea what's happening to him?" asked Mitzy.

Barb circled, did a loop the loop then smiled. "I'm afraid I do, yes. Biskit has inhaled a scent that has made his mind a prisoner of Dimension Pong," she said.

"Dimension Pong?" repeated Commander F.

"Oh, I've heard of that," said Example One. "I thought it was called the Pong Dimension."

"Well, I think Dimension Pong sounds better," said Barb. "But it doesn't matter. It is a part of the universe where smell is more important than any of the other senses."

"It's so nice to have someone on my level," said Barb, lowering herself so she was face to face with the pink mouse.

"I don't know a great deal about it," said Example One.

"No one does." Barb wiggled one of her fins and suddenly the room darkened.

The others were used to Barb's abilities but Neville crouched down in fear as a thousand stars filled the room. The stars swirled around, giving the impression that the room was zooming through space. It stopped in front of a circle of darkness, surrounded by bright-coloured lights.

"Who can tell me what this is?" asked Barb.

"It's a quasar – bright luminous gases surrounding a black hole at the centre," said Example One.

"Correct," said Barb. "The only way to reach the Pong Dimension is to travel through one of these and, since travelling through black holes is extremely dangerous, very little is known about what lies on the other side."

"Cheeeeeese," moaned Biskit.

"It appears to be cheese," said Commander F.

"Yes," said Barb.

"Noooo," groaned Biskit.

Mitzy looked at him anxiously. "How do we get him back?" she asked.

Barb blinked her eyes and the room lightened again. She swam up, her surrounding water swishing around her as she moved, sending splashes to the floor. She arrived back at her bowl and dropped inside.

SPLOSH!

"There are some questions even I cannot answer," she said. "The Pong Dimension has its own smell-based laws of physics."

"There is so much we don't know about the universe," said Example One.

Mitzy lifted her right leg and began to clean herself as she thought about how to save her partner. "You said the smell put him in this state," she said. "Maybe that's what we need to bring him out of it."

"Interesting idea," said Example One. "You mean some kind of a counter-smell."

"Would that work?" asked Commander F.

"I'm so confused," said Neville.

"Yes, that could work," said Barb. "But it would need to be strong enough to get through to the part of his brain connected with his memory."

"Something familiar?" said Mitzy. She switched to her left leg but as she did so she felt a movement in her stomach, which gave her an idea. "So it doesn't have to be a nice smell?"

"It's probably better if it's not," said Example One. "Smell can be a powerful memory-trigger."

"Agent Mitzy, what are you thinking?" asked Commander F, inspecting the chewed remains of his radish leaves to see if there was anything left worth eating.

"I don't understand any of what you're saying," said Neville.

"I need a smell that will draw him out of his cheese-mare into the real world," said Mitzy. "Something strong, something familiar." She turned to look at Commander F and Example One. "I think you may all want to leave," she said.

"Now, Agent Mitzy, you don't give the orders here," said Commander F. "We need to see if this works."

"Yes, it will be fascinating," said Example One.

"See if what works?" asked Neville.

"Oh, very well," said Mitzy. "But don't say I didn't warn you."

Mitzy turned around so that her bottom was directly over Biskit's nose. She raised her tail and let rip.

"Oh, I see," said the pug, attempting to block his nose, but he was too late.

CHAPTER 7

🐾

A SMELLY AWAKENING

Biskit was trapped in a cheesy nightmare. He tried to move his legs but they were stuck in a pool of gooey yellow gunk. The more he struggled to escape, the faster it pulled him down. A raft of hard cheddar drifted by. He tried to grab it but it crumbled between his paws. Above him, a towering volcano erupted, sending clouds of yellow smoke into the air. Molten lava of melted cheese dripped down into the pool.

He opened his mouth to cry out but cheese poured in, overwhelming his senses. He was alone in his horror. The soft cheese

was flowing into his mouth and his nose. He felt as though he was drowning in smell.

Then the colours darkened. Another scent had entered his nostrils. It was a smell he recognized. It sent his mind reeling and got his nostrils twitching. He followed the smell up and out of the cheese world and opened his eyes.

Mitzy, Example One, Commander F and Neville were standing over him. He looked up at the posters of sick animals and the bookshelf with the familiar round goldfish bowl.

"Biskit." Mitzy's look of relief was tinged with embarrassment. As Biskit realized what the smell was, he understood why.

"I never thought I'd be grateful for you doing that," he said.

Mitzy smiled and let out an apologetic purr.

"Welcome back," said Barb.

"How are you feeling?" asked Commander F, with surprising softness in his voice.

"Like a stink bomb just exploded in my

nose," said Biskit, "but I think I'm all right."

"Good," said Commander F. "THEN STOP LYING AROUND AND GET BACK TO WORK!"

Startled, Biskit jumped to his feet, wagging his tail. "Yes, sir, I'm ready. We need to stop this cheese before it attacks again."

"I'm not sure it is attacking," said Example One.

"Not attacking? It knocked me out," Biskit scoffed.

"And Philip and his mother," said Mitzy.

"And my owners," added Neville.

"Maybe the smell is a form of self defence, like with a skunk," said Example One.

"Nonsense," said Commander F. "Biskit is right. This alien cheese has infiltrated our planet and now it's waging war on us. We must strike back."

Barb sighed. "If you treat everyone like an

enemy, how will you ever make more friends?"
she asked. "Remember, I am an alien visitor,
too."

"Yes, but you don't knock out innocent
humans." Commander F dropped his radish
and stamped on it angrily.

"Barb has a point, though," said Mitzy,
remembering what Daley had said about the
Pet Defenders always assuming the worst of
the aliens that arrived. "What if they aren't
attacking? Every time one of these things has
struck, it has immediately left the scene—"

"Because it doesn't want to get caught," said
Commander F.

"Or it wants to hide," said Mitzy.

"Hide where?" demanded Commander F.

"Remember the picnic bench where Neville's
owners were knocked out?" said Biskit. "There
was a book there, too. It was hollowed out as
though something had been inside."

Mitzy felt the hairs on her back stand on end as the thought struck her. "Neville, did your owners go anywhere besides the cheese shop?"

"Yes," said Neville. "They went to the library."

"The library next door?" said Mitzy. "Why didn't you tell us this before?"

"You didn't ask," said Neville.

Biskit's eyes met his partner's. "We need to go," he said. "Neville, stay with Example One. Help him find a smell to wake up your owners."

"Good idea," said Commander F.

"Yes," said Example One, adjusting his glasses, "although if you're using the same technique that Mitzy used, I may watch from behind a glass this time."

CHAPTER 8

❧

THE HOLEY HOLY

Nothington-on-Sea's library was only open until lunchtime on Saturdays so it was locked when the Pet Defenders arrived. Biskit suggested they find a way round the back but Mitzy paused in the small yard behind the cheese shop. A white overall hung from the washing line. Mitzy sprang up and tugged at one corner. It flopped to the ground, landing on top of her. She wriggled free.

"What are you doing?" asked Biskit.

Mitzy nudged a peg with her nose. "Come here," she said.

"Why?" Biskit asked.

"You've seen what happens when you smell this stuff. Give us your nose."

"Won't that hurt?" asked Biskit.

Mitzy took the peg between her teeth. Biskit hopped down and approached reluctantly.

"I'm not sure about this."

"Don't be such a scaredy-dog," said Mitzy.

Biskit moved his nose closer and Mitzy clamped the peg over it.

"YeeEEAAOUCH!" he yelled.

"Quiet," said Mitzy.

"My nose is a finely tuned instrument," stated Biskit.

"Not a washing line."

"Come on, you need to do mine now," said Mitzy.

"With pleasure." Biskit picked up a peg in his mouth. Mitzy leaned in and he snapped it shut on her nose.

Mitzy instantly
understood why Biskit
had cried out. The pain
was excruciating.

"All fine?" asked Biskit,
knowing it wasn't.

"Yes, of course, let's go," said Mitzy.

They jumped over the wall and Mitzy
approached the library's back door.

"It's locked…" she said.

"Leave this to me." Biskit jumped up on
to a windowsill, only to find that it was shut
tight. He tried to make another jump to
the next floor up but missed and fell to the
ground.

"Biskit—" began Mitzy.

"Not a problem," said Biskit. "I'll shimmy
up the old—" He jumped and grabbed the
drainpipe but it wasn't very well attached

to the wall and fell away. Biskit crashed to the ground with the plastic piping clattering everywhere.

"Biskit," hissed Mitzy.

"What?" he snapped.

"What I was going to say was that the door is locked but there's a cat flap."

"Oh, yes. Now you mention it, the library did used to have a cat. He was called Wordsworth. They had a tortoise, too, called Shelley."

"Biskit, shush," said Mitzy.

With the lights off and the blinds drawn, it was dark inside. The Pet Defenders stepped into the main library where a large round skylight lit up the dust that hung in the air. Mitzy looked around at the shelves of books.

"So where would you hide if you were an alien cheese?" said Biskit.

"The food section?" said Mitzy, stopping by a shelf with titles such as *Posh Cooking* by Gordon

Bleurgh, *Speedy Cookery* by Mike Rowave and *Grilling Cheese* by Hal Oomy.

Biskit approached the books and lowered his nose, then stopped. "How can I find them if I can't sniff them out?"

Mitzy reached up and pulled a book off the bottom shelf. It fell open. There was nothing inside. She was about to reach for another when a book on a higher shelf wriggled forwards then dropped to the ground. Biskit and Mitzy stepped back and watched as the cover slowly opened and a round lump of cheese flew out, its arms raised. It had yellow pock-holed rind and it hovered just off the ground. A pair of eyes peered out of two of the holes.

The cheese buzzed about, making a series of squelches and raspberries then landed on its two spindly legs and moved closer, scrutinizing them with its tiny eyes.

"I am Holey Holy, leader of the cheeses of the Pong Dimension, descendent of Gouda the Good and Feta the Better. I greet you on behalf of my people." The alien waved its arms in the air as it spoke.

"What are you talking about?" asked Biskit.

"Biskit! Show some respect," said Mitzy. She turned to face the cheese and bowed. "Holey Holy," she said. "This is our planet and we are its defenders."

"Yes, I know. It is written," said Holey Holy. "You are here to fulfill your destiny and save us." The alien put its hands together in thanks.

"How can we be sure it is them?" croaked another voice as a second cheese stepped out of a book about Japanese cuisine by Sue Sheerole. This cheese had a belt of thick red rind round its middle and walked using its staff to steady itself. "The *Book of Cheese* said nothing about our saviours being such strange hairy beasts."

"High Stinker," said Holey Holy. "You must trust in the word, for the word is cheese. Yay, it is written in the *Book of Cheese* that our defenders will greet us when we find the Mother Home – and here they are."

"The Mother Home?" said Mitzy. "This is Earth, our planet."

"And we are not your defenders," snarled Biskit. "I think you've got the wrong end of the stick. We're here to send you back where you came from, not help you."

"Ha, it is you who has the wrong end of the cheese stick," said High Stinker. "This is our home."

"Is that why you attacked the humans?" said Biskit. "My owner is still trapped in the Pong Dimension."

"Our aroma has an unfortunate side effect for you carbon-based life forms," said Holey Holy calmly. "We deeply regret these accidents, caused by some of our less-mature members."

"What does that mean?" asked Mitzy.

"My cheese congregation," proclaimed Holey Holy. "Come forth. Show yourselves."

All around the library, more varieties of cheese emerged from hollowed-out books and hovered closer.

"**Noooooooom**," they hummed, in perfect harmony.

"Baby Bell," called Holey Holy. "Nibbles, don't be shy. Join us."

Two smaller cheeses came forwards. One of them was tiny with big eyes. The other, Biskit recognized as the one who had knocked him out.

"Baby Bell found himself in public when his hiding place was removed, while Nibbles fell asleep in the shop next door and awoke to find he was about to be consumed," said Holey Holy.

"Why have you come here?" asked Mitzy. "Why do you call it the Mother Home?"

"Because that is what it is," said Holey Holy.

"**Noooooooommmmm**," sang the cheeses.

Had it not been for the pegs, Biskit and Mitzy wouldn't have stood a chance. Even with them on, they were aware of the incredible smell.

"The *Book of Cheese* has led us here," said High Stinker. "After many thousands of years, we have finally returned to the big cheese, our Mother Home."

"Let us remember the words of the *Book of Cheese*," said Holey Holy before bursting into song in a low velvety voice:

"The Mother Home will be found
On the ground that goes around
The third planet from the sun
Of the Milky Way where we begun."

"What is that supposed to mean?" asked Biskit.

"It means that they come from Earth," said

Mitzy. "We're the third planet and we go around the sun in the Milky Way."

"I do not believe they are here to protect us," said High Stinker. "I say we test the prophecy and see if they can withstand our holy stench. All cheese is great."

"Let it never be grated," chanted the other cheeses.

"No," said Holey Holy. "We must not attack our defenders."

But High Stinker cried, "Cheese congregation, remove their nose plugs. How can they defend us if our odour defeats them?"

"**Nooooooooommmmm**…"

The cheeses moved forwards, fixing their beady eyes menacingly on Biskit and Mitzy as an overpowering aroma seeped out of their pores.

CHAPTER 9

CHEESE HIBERNATION

The cheeses were getting closer. The Pet Defenders' pegs were still in place but Biskit and Mitzy wouldn't be able to keep them on while fighting the cheeses. Mitzy could already feel hers slipping. As soon as they pinged off, the Pet Defenders would be exposed to the toxic stink and lost in the Pong Dimension.

"This is our Mother Home. You cannot stand in our way," said High Stinker.

"No, they are our friends," said Holey Holy.

"It's true, we mean you no harm," said Mitzy.

"Speak for yourself," growled Biskit. "If I'm about to be attacked by a room full of angry cheeses, I'm taking some of them with me."

It was a hopeless situation. The numerous varieties of cheese were so close that they would soon knock the pegs off. Mitzy pushed hers down with one paw but she knew she wouldn't be able to defend herself and keep it on. She took a deep intake of breath. She was wondering how long she could hold it when a voice cried, "Stop!"

Biskit, Mitzy and all of the cheeses turned to see a fox with patchy red fur jump on to a table.

"Daley," said Biskit.

"Hi, Biskit," replied the fox. "Are these cheeses disagreeing with you?"

"What are you up to, you sly fox?" said Biskit.

"I consider that offensive," said Daley. "I should leave them to it. But that's my problem. I care too much." Then he cried,

"Cheeses of the Pong Dimension, all cheese is great."

"Let us never be grated," chanted the cheeses.

"Stand down and leave these ignorant natives be," said Daley.

"These what?" said Biskit.

"Biskit," hissed Mitzy. "Look."

"**Nooooommmmmm**." The cheeses were retreating and returning to their hiding places on the bookshelves. Within a matter of seconds, Holey Holy and High Stinker were the only two remaining.

"Daley," snarled Biskit. "Is this all your doing?"

"I just saved you from a room full of deadly cheese and you still can't bring yourself to say thank you," said Daley.

"Thank you," said Mitzy, adjusting her peg. "Hey, why aren't you affected by the stink?"

"No sense of smell, remember?" said Daley, tapping his nose and winking.

"What are you up to?" demanded Biskit.

"Daley is our guide," said Holey Holy. "He is helping us."

Biskit snarled at the fox. "You'd better start talking."

"They arrived last week through a portal down on the beach. That Martian came through the same one," said Daley.

"Why didn't you tell us this when we saw you?" asked Mitzy.

"Yes, what are you getting out of this?" said Biskit.

"Nothing," said Daley. "I felt sorry for them. I've always had a soft spot for cheese and I thought I could find them somewhere to hibernate before you lot charged in all gung-ho."

"Gung-ho?" said Biskit.

"Hibernate?" said Mitzy.

"Yes, it is our time," said High Stinker. "But we must find a safe place to sleep."

"I keep telling you. We no longer need to hibernate now we have reached the Mother Home," said Holey Holy. "We are safe here with our defenders."

"We are not your defenders," said Biskit.

Without warning, Holey Holy burst into song again, waving his arms wildly as he sang:

"The Cheeses' saviours you will know
When they deny that they are so
They'll refuse to befriend us,
Our heroes are the Cheese Defenders."

"I know he sounds like he's a couple of crackers short of a selection box," said Daley, "but they need our help. Once they go into hibernation they grow a thick rind around them like a cocoon. It contains the smell."

"So that's why the humans weren't knocked out until the outer casing came off," said Mitzy.

"Yes, I thought the library would be a good hiding spot," said Daley. "The books contain their smell while humans are around. It wasn't my fault that someone took out the book where Baby Bell was hiding. And how was I to know that Nibbles would sneak next door for a snooze in the cheese shop? I'm the one trying to help these poor frightened cheeses."

Biskit and Mitzy looked at each other. "Frightened?" said Mitzy.

"Frightened of what?" said Biskit.

Holey Holy sighed. "There used to be many more of us," he said. "Our numbers would have filled a thousand of these rooms." A small yellow tear squeezed itself out of his eye. "But over the years we have been hunted. We are most vulnerable during hibernation."

"Hunted?" said Mitzy. "What in its right mind would hunt cheese that smells like you? No offence meant."

"None taken," said Holey Holy. "We pride ourselves on our smell."

"When we left the Pong Dimension with the intention of returning to our Mother Home, we first had to travel through a black hole," said High Stinker. "It was there our pursuer picked up our scent."

"What pursuer?" asked Mitzy.

"It lives on the edges of a black hole. It is called a Quasar Mouse," said Holey Holy.

"**Nooooomm**," chanted the cheeses fearfully.

"Ha. I think I can handle a little mouse," said Mitzy, licking her lips.

"Unfortunately this one is larger than the rodents on this planet," said Holey Holy. "In fact, it is larger than any of your Earth creatures."

"So big that our smell has no effect on it except to make it even hungrier," said High Stinker.

"The Quasar Mouse has followed us across the universe for many years. But now we have stopped running. Here in the Mother Home the Quasar Mouse will be defeated and we will be free. You, our Cheese Defenders, will save us."

"We are not Cheese Defenders." Biskit turned to Daley. "This is your fault. You should have made them go back where they came from as soon as they arrived."

"And send them into the jaws of the Quasar Mouse?" said Daley.

"Well, no, but—" began Biskit.

"Hold on —" said Mitzy — "if they're being hunted, what's to say this Quasar Mouse won't follow them here?"

"Well, yes, exactly. That's the thing I need to talk to you about," said Daley.

The Pet Defenders slowly turned to face him.

"The portal these cheeses came through is still open. They usually close straight away but this one is getting bigger."

"Bigger?" said Mitzy. "Where is this portal then?"

"On the beach," said Daley. "That's what I was doing when I saw you. I've been keeping an eye on it in case anything else comes through but nothing has yet. It's almost as though whatever is on the other side is making it bigger…" Daley looked shiftily at Biskit, then at Mitzy and finally at Holey Holy.

"The Quasar Mouse," said Holey Holy.

"We need to get you off this planet," said Daley.

"No," said Holey Holy. "Destiny has brought us here. This is our Mother Home. I will not lead our people away now."

"We cannot defend ourselves against the Quasar Mouse," said High Stinker. "It would be folly to face our foe. We will do what we do best. We will hide, then grow shells that will keep us from being hunted."

"**Noooooomm**." From the way the cheese congregation hovered around and moved behind High Stinker, it was clear that they agreed with him.

"Daley," said Mitzy. "Keep this cheese under wraps. We don't want any more humans getting knocked out. Biskit and I will go to the beach."

"And why would I follow your orders?" asked Daley.

"Because you're responsible for all this," said Biskit.

"Yes, I suppose that's fair," the foc admitted, hanging his head. "Also, I don't think I fancy facing this Quasar Mouse. The portal is the biggest I've ever seen."

"I will not remain here in this cold dark place," said Holey Holy. "I will go and face our enemy alongside the Cheese Defenders."

"Pet Defenders," said Biskit.

"It doesn't matter what we're called. We need to get to the beach and quickly," said Mitzy.

"**Noooooooommm**," chanted the cheeses as Holey Holy sang:

"When we reach the Mother Home
No more shall we have to roam
Every chunk, lump and slice,
Safe in a blue cheese paradise."

"That's all very well," said Biskit, "except this isn't your home and because of you, it's not safe."

"Don't worry," said Mitzy. "This is what we do best. The Quasar Mouse won't be eating cheese on our watch."

CHAPTER 10

🐾

THE QUASAR MOUSE

Biskit and Mitzy knew something was wrong as soon as they stepped out of the library. There was such panic in the air of Nothington-on-Sea that none of the fleeing humans noticed the dog, cat and flying alien cheese heading in the opposite direction. Biskit and Mitzy kept Holey Holy as far from the humans as possible but a couple got too close and dropped to the ground.

When they reached the promenade they saw the cause of the mass hysteria. A mouse the size of an ocean liner was wading through the shallow waters. Its wiry whiskers skimmed the top of the waves as it twitched its huge nose. When it raised its front legs out of the water, it revealed claws as long as cutlasses. It swished its tail and sent huge waves crashing on to the pebble beach. It opened its mouth and let out a deafening

"SQUEEAAK!"

Biskit, Mitzy and Holey Holy stopped to stare.

"The Quasar Mouse," said the hovering cheese.

A seagull landed next to them with Example

One on its back. Both the bird and pink mouse had masks protecting them from the smell of the cheese. "How remarkable, a Quasar Mouse. It's a female, if I'm not mistaken," said Example One, looking over the top of his glasses at the approaching creature. "Apparently it's the electromagnetic radiation of their environment that causes them to grow so large."

The Quasar Mouse sniffed and slowly turned her huge head towards them.

"She can smell the cheese," said Mitzy.

"I have no fear," said Holey Holy. "I am with my protectors."

The mouse lowered her nose to the beach and sniffed, drawing clumps of pebbles and sand into her nostrils. She then exhaled, firing them out again. Example One's seagull took to the air while the Pet Defenders ducked behind the promenade wall. The stones clattered against the bricks like machine-gun bullets. Holey Holy would have been pelted had Mitzy not grabbed him with her tail and dragged him to safety.

"I thank you," he said.

"So what's our plan?" asked Biskit.

Mitzy peeked over the top of the wall. Behind the mouse was a large patch of strangely shimmering sky. It was the biggest portal Mitzy had ever seen.

"We need to get the mouse to go back through that," she said.

Example One typed furiously into his tablet, squinting at the screen. "The portal is closing," he said.

"Can you keep it open?" asked Mitzy.

"That is an interesting question to ponder," said Example One, tapping his head with his stylus.

"Ponder quickly," said Mitzy.

"Portals are created by small rips in the fabric of reality," said Example One. "Up until this point we have been concentrating our efforts on finding ways of detecting them and closing them. I've never considered how I could keep one open. I suppose if we were to tweak the portal identifier we could—"

"We don't need the details," interrupted Biskit. "How long do you need?"

"Ten minutes," said Example One.

Most of the humans who had been on the beach that afternoon had run off screaming at

the first sight of the Quasar Mouse. Only one man remained. He was holding his phone up, trying to capture the incredible scene on video. Normally, the Pet Defenders would have targeted him with Forget-Me-Plop, but since this would have made him a sitting target for the approaching mouse, the order had not yet been given.

"You get that man out of harm's way," said Mitzy. "I'll keep the mouse busy."

"How?" said Biskit.

"Trust me," said Mitzy. "It won't be the first mouse I've played with."

"Ahem. I am here, you know," said Example One.

"Sorry," said Mitzy.

"What about me?" asked Holey Holy. "What shall you have me do?"

"Stay here," said Mitzy, pushing him down with her paw.

"And try not to get eaten," said Biskit.

CHAPTER 11

🐾

MOUSE AND CAT

Mitzy ran down the stone steps on to the beach. The Quasar Mouse sniffed, once again causing a mini tornado with her nostrils. Mitzy paused in front of the alien, steadying herself with her tail. The mouse swung her head down, sending a pile of pebbles into the air with her long whiskers. Mitzy darted through the stony downpour and saw that she had got the Quasar Mouse's attention.

"My tail," she muttered. "Holey Holy's scent must have rubbed off on it."

The Quasar Mouse was so large, she was struggling to see the source of the smell.

Mitzy took her opportunity and ran.

"**SQUEEEEAAAK!**"

The mouse's terrible cry echoed off the hotels and restaurants that lined Nothington-on-Sea's coastal road. Mitzy could hear the screams of the human observers but she couldn't worry about that now. She had a job to do.

"Hey, Minnie," she yelled. "Over here."

Mitzy took a zigzagged route across the beach, managing to stay just out of the Quasar Mouse's reach. She got a feeling that, in spite of her size, this mouse was not the smartest creature in the universe.

Furious with frustration, the Quasar Mouse pounced, bringing her huge clawed foot down on top of Mitzy.

The cat wriggled out of her grip then sunk her own claws into the side of the Quasar Mouse's face.

"SQUEEAAK!"

roared the giant rodent.
In her time working as a Pet
Defender, Mitzy had experienced
her fair share of terrifying and bizarre
encounters. There had been a colossal dung
beetle, alien beards, snot snatchers and burping
shapeshifters. But she had fought all of these
battles alongside Biskit. This time she was on

her own. The Quasar Mouse moved towards her, swishing her snake-like tail across the pebble beach.

"Come on then. Let's play," yelled Mitzy.

"**SQUEEEEAAAK!**" The mouse charged.
KRUNCH-KRUNCH-KRUNCH!

Mitzy tried to put some distance between them but the Quasar Mouse dug her nose under a pile of pebbles and sent them up into the air again. Mitzy changed direction but this meant she was now moving towards her pursuer.

"**SQUEEEEEAAAK!**"

Mitzy was reminded of the first time she ever caught a mouse. She remembered being suddenly faced with a poor little petrified creature. Mitzy had no desire to eat it, but simply letting it go would have made the whole chase seem pointless. To her shame, Mitzy had played with the mouse, teasing and tormenting it, trapping its tail and releasing it over and over again. She had let it go eventually but she had never forgotten the incident and she doubted that the mouse had.

As the enormous space rodent caught Mitzy's tail under her claw, the cat understood how that poor little mouse had felt.

"Get off me," she meowed desperately.

This felt like payback.

The Quasar Mouse released her and she scrambled across the beach. But she turned her head, skimming her huge blade-like whiskers towards Mitzy's legs. Mitzy leaped into the air and did a backwards somersault to avoid the attack, but one of the razor-sharp whiskers caught the end of her tail.

"**YEEEOUCH!**" she screeched. She landed back on the beach but lost her footing as each of the mouse's thunderous steps caused mini earthquakes.

Mitzy was trapped. The mouse's huge head moved down towards her. The fearsome creature's great jaws closed round Mitzy's collar. The Quasar Mouse lifted her head and Mitzy felt herself dragged into the air. She kicked her legs and waved her tail but she couldn't free herself. The Quasar Mouse tipped her head back, tossing Mitzy into the air and opening her jaws.

"**WEEOooOW!**" yelped Mitzy.

She spread her legs wide, managing to latch her claws on to the upper and lower rows of the mouse's teeth, preventing her from dropping into the creature's throat. She clenched her leg muscles and sprang up

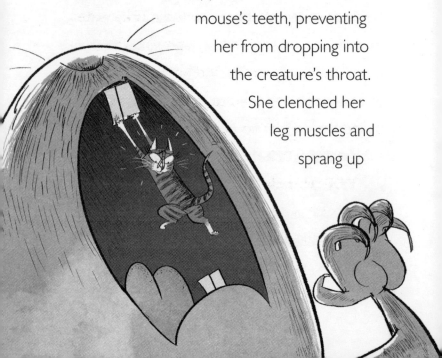

into the air, then swished her tail so that she landed on the Quasar Mouse's whiskers. Sliding down them, she felt like she was rolling over a bed of cutlasses.

"**SCHReeeOUCH!**" she cried as she fell towards the beach.

The mouse tipped back on to her hind legs and tried to grab Mitzy. Her right paw missed but her left one caught the cat on the back of her head, sending her spinning over towards the grey frothing waves.

Mitzy splashed down into the murky water. Even if she had known how to swim, the current was too strong. It dragged her back. She surfaced and tried to breathe but was pulled back under so quickly that she drew salty water into her lungs.

"**YEEOUrck!**"

She spat out the seawater as she came up again. Great waves with white tips crashed over her. She was powerless against the tide.

Then she heard a voice.

"It's OK. I've got you."

Biskit hauled her back to safety.

CHAPTER 12

·:·

SACRIFICIAL CHEESE

The man filming the incredible scene on his camera phone had actually come to the beach hoping to find something interesting with his metal detector. Standing rooted to the spot, phone held up and metal detector lying on the ground, he didn't spare a thought for his safety. He may have never found a Roman coin like some of his friends but which one of them could claim to have filmed a giant mouse?

He was so caught up in what he was doing that he didn't notice the dog until it was right in front of him. It barked then jumped up and snatched the phone in its jaws.

"Noo!" yelped the man.

The scruffy mongrel jerked its head, throwing the device in the air. The man watched helplessly as it smashed on the beach. Then the dog jumped up again and pushed him with his paws.

"Hey!" he yelled.

As he stumbled back, he saw the mouse's huge tail sweep across the beach. If it hadn't been for the dog, the tail would have caught him. Instead, it was the mongrel who was whisked away and sent flying into the crashing waves.

The man didn't pause to consider why the dog had saved his life or whether the brave animal was all right. He turned and sprinted for the steps. When he reached the promenade, he stopped and looked back at the giant mouse. It was the most incredible sight he had ever witnessed and, even without the footage on his phone, he would still be able to tell everyone what happened.

Or so he thought.

SHHHPLAT!

Something white landed on the man's head, wiping away the memory of his close encounter with the Quasar Mouse.

Biskit and Mitzy crawled up the beach, out of the waves. Biskit shook the water from his fur and Mitzy caught her breath.

"Thank you," she said.

"Any time," said Biskit, spitting out a piece of seaweed. "Now we need to get that mouse back down that hole before she eats the cheese."

However, Holey Holy had emerged from his hiding space and was hovering across the beach. His arms were spread and his eyes were closed. "**Noooooooom**," he hummed as he came to a standstill. Then he sang:

*"We will bring our enemy to its knees
In the final battle of the cheese
But before we reach our paradise
There must be a sacrifice."*

"What does that mean?" asked Mitzy.

"Who cares," said Biskit. "He needs to move out of the way."

The Pet Defenders weren't the only ones to have noticed the cheese. The Quasar Mouse let out a deafening **SQUEEEEAAAK** and began her lumbering approach down the beach.

"HOLEY HOLY, GET OUT OF THE WAY!" yelled Mitzy.

But the cheese was not moving. He smiled serenely and said, "You have your path. I have mine. I must do that which must be done."

"He's going to sacrifice himself," said Mitzy.

The mouse stumbled on the uneven shifting pebbles but didn't pause for long. Nothing was going to stop it.

"I'll get him," said Biskit.

"But our pegs have gone," said Mitzy, realizing hers must have flown off when she hit the water.

"I'll hold my breath," said Biskit. "I'll get Holey Holy to the portal. You need to make sure the Quasar Mouse goes through."

Biskit turned and ran towards the cheese. He jumped up and snatched Holey Holy in his teeth just as the Quasar Mouse was about to do the same. The creature's huge nose smacked against the beach. Mitzy ducked from the raining pebbles. When she looked up again she had lost sight of Biskit.

"Biskit!" she yelled.

The Quasar Mouse raised her mighty head, revealing Biskit running down the beach towards the shimmering patch of sky. The Quasar Mouse took chase.

Example One brought his seagull swooping down and landed in the shallow water next to Mitzy.

"The portal is ready," he said, clutching his tablet. "But I've never experienced one this large. I'm concerned that by keeping it open I am increasing the danger of something else coming through it."

"What does that mean?" asked Mitzy.

"It means that if we don't close it soon, we could be overrun with Quasar Mice."

"We'll get her through it," said Mitzy. "Keep it open."

She took after the Quasar Mouse, avoiding the flying pebbles and her huge swinging tail. She couldn't tell if Biskit was managing to stay ahead of the mouse but she hoped she could get there in time to help.

CHAPTER 13

❀

MOUSE HOLE

Biskit could hear the **KKKiRANCH! KKKiRANCH!** of the Quasar Mouse. He could feel her cold breath on his back. Her huge head cast a shadow that blocked out the dying orange light of the sunset. But the only thing Biskit could smell was the cheese.

"This is how the *Book of Cheese* tells it," cried Holey Holy. "You truly are the defender of the cheeses."

Biskit wanted to argue but he was holding the cheese in his jaws, trying not to inhale its scent. It was impossible. He tried to keep his feet steady and his mind calm but he could feel reality drifting away.

The pungent stench burned through his nostril hairs and made his brain feel foggy and distant. It was awful. Biskit stumbled and felt his eyelids droop.

The **SPLASH** of the water under his paws reminded him of the hellish visions of cheese he had experienced in the Pong Dimension. He had to focus on what was real.

"**SQUEEEEEAAAK!**"

The Quasar Mouse, thought Biskit. That was real enough. He flapped his ears against his eyes, trying to keep himself from drifting off.

"From this portal our enemy came and so it shall return again," proclaimed Holey Holy.

Biskit was trying to concentrate. He was close to the portal now. It was just above the crest of the waves. He ran deeper into the frothing sea. He doubled his efforts. He had to keep up enough speed to ensure that the

Quasar Mouse didn't realize what was happening until it was too late. But Biskit's eyes were failing him.

The setting sun had turned from orange to yellow. Cheese clouded his vision. His legs gave way and he dropped into the water. The last thing he felt was Holey Holy slip out from his jaws and fly up and away into the shimmering gateway.

The Quasar Mouse didn't pause for thought. She followed the cheese.

Back on the shore, Mitzy watched as the huge mouse vanished into the portal.

"She's gone," said Example One, his seagull hovering above Mitzy. "The portal is closing now."

Mitzy looked around frantically. "Where's Biskit?" she said.

"I'm not sure. I lost sight of him in all the excitement," replied Example One. "I think the cheese went through the portal."

"Biskit!" Mitzy meowed at the ocean. "Biskit!"

She couldn't avoid the thought that this would be the moment where one of his stupid, reckless and amazingly brave acts finally got the better of him.

"Biskit," she yelled, bounding into the sea without a thought for her own safety.

Had Biskit suffered the same fate as his partner and fallen through a portal? Was this the end?

"BISKIT!" she cried.

Then she saw something floating in the white foam of the waves. She dived in and kicked her legs, all fear blocked out by a tiny glimmer of hope. She swallowed mouthfuls of water but, through sheer determination, her jaws connected with the scruff of Biskit's neck. She hauled him back to the beach.

He coughed, then opened his eyes.

"I couldn't save Holey Holy," he said.

"You saved us," said Mitzy.

"You mean, *we* did," said Biskit.

Up on the promenade, the humans who had witnessed the Quasar Mouse's rampage stood covered in sticky white Forget-Me-Plop, wondering why they were staring at the sea, or pointing at the clouds. They also wondered why they were all covered in bird poop.

"Someone should do something about these birds," said a man, wagging his finger. "It's a disgrace."

"What are those animals doing on the beach? Dogs are supposed to be kept on leads," said another. "I say, where's my metal detector?"

"Is that mouse sitting on a seagull?" asked a woman, mouth and eyes wide with disbelief. "Oh, I've been hit again," she added, feeling another squelchy white splat on her head.

CHAPTER 14

THE MOTHER HOME

Once the cover-up mission was under way, Biskit and Mitzy returned to the library. Example One supplied them with protective masks and Commander F told them through a seagull communicator that they had better wrap up this cheese situation quickly. It was dark by the time they stepped inside, where they found the cheeses gathered around, harmonizing somberly.

"**Nooooommm...**"

Daley was curled up on a pile of picture books. He stood up when he saw the Pet Defenders enter.

"So what happened?" he asked. "Saved the day again, I take it?"

The cheeses fell silent but High Stinker stepped forwards, held his staff aloft and said, "Where is Holey Holy?"

Mitzy looked at the alien cheese, hoping he would be able to see the answer in her eyes but High Stinker was either unable or unwilling to read her expression. "What?" he said. "Where is our leader?"

"He didn't make it," said Biskit. "He led the Quasar Mouse into the portal. He saved your people. He was the Cheese Defender, not us."

"Oh, sorrowful day," High Stinker wailed as he looked up at the skylight, raising his palms. "Holey Holy has been taken to the great cheeseboard in the sky."

"**Noooooommmm...**" the cheeses chanted and High Stinker sang:

"One cheese, one life, one sacrifice
To save the cheeses from the mice
Then to the Mother Home they'll go
And leave their friends down below."

His voice was higher than Holey Holy's but just as tuneful.

"Leave the defenders down below?" said Biskit. "What does that mean?"

He turned to see Mitzy cleaning herself again. She was thinking. "High Stinker, what was the verse about the Mother Home that Holey Holy told us at the start?"

"**Noooooommmm**." The cheeses accompanied High Stinker as he sang:

"The Mother Home will be found
On the ground that goes around
The third planet from the sun
Of the Milky Way where we begun."

"It does sound like it means Earth," said Biskit.

"No, it doesn't," said Mitzy. "It says the Mother Home will be found on the ground that goes *around* the third planet."

"Which means…" began Daley.

"The moon." Biskit finished off the thought.

Mitzy nodded. "It's talking about the moon."

"What is this moon?" asked High Stinker.

Mitzy looked up at the full moon shining through the skylight of the library. "That," she said.

High Stinker looked up, then dropped to his knees. "Behold, cheeses, that is the Mother Home, the big cheese," said High Stinker. "It is just as it is drawn in the *Book of Cheese*. Look."

"**Moooooonnnnnn**," chanted the cheeses.

The two smaller cheeses, Baby Bell and Nibbles, carried a book between them, bright

yellow and covered in a strange lettering. High
Stinker opened it to a page with a picture of
the moon.

"The *Book of Cheese* talks of the great Cheese Grating when our Mother Home was hit." The next page showed a comet hitting the moon and fragments breaking off. "Our people were carried away in the comet's tail and dragged across the galaxy, then through a black hole into the Pong Dimension."

"Sorry. Are you telling us that the moon is actually made of cheese?" said Biskit.

"Yes, and so we shall return. Cheeses, let us go home to Mother." High Stinker raised his staff in the air and drifted up towards the skylight.

"**Mooooooon**."

The rest of the cheese congregation did the same.

"Er, that's glass you're heading for," warned Mitzy.

But her words couldn't be heard under the chanting of the cheese.

"I think you might want to take cover," said Daley.

"Good call," said Biskit.

When High Stinker reached the skylight, he whacked it with his staff. It cracked, then as the rest of the cheeses collided with the glass, it shattered. Biskit, Mitzy and Daley took shelter under piles of books as the glass rained down on them. By the time the final shard had fallen, the cheeses were way up high, lost in the night sky.

The chanting was distant, although Mitzy wondered if it had changed to "**Thank yoooooooooouuuuuu**."

Biskit and Mitzy pulled off their masks.

"That's that then," said Daley, turning to go, only to find the Pet Defenders blocking his way. He took a step back. "Come on, I helped out. Besides, I was only trying to do the right thing."

"Daley, if you have the ability to sense when portals appear, you need to work with us," said Mitzy.

"With you?" said Daley.

"With us?" said Biskit.

"Yes," said Mitzy. "These alien invasions are getting more and more common. We need someone on our side who can help us stop them before they start. And someone who won't always think the worst of our visitors."

"Sorry." Daley shook his head. "I work alone."

Mitzy looked at Biskit. "Biskit said the same thing when we first met."

Biskit smiled. "She's right. It's time to help us. I have a feeling we're going to need all the help we can get soon."

"Including help from a no-good, bin-bothering scavenger like me?" said Daley.

"Yes," said Mitzy. "This is our planet. It

belongs to us all, humans and animals, every one of us."

"And it's down to us to protect it," said Biskit.

At that, all three animals looked up at the twinkling stars in the night sky, wondering what fresh marvels the universe had in store for them. Whatever they were, the Pet Defenders would be there to save the day.